DAMAGED

Jen

glad you are my sister.

love *[signature]*

Other books by Phlip Arima

poetry
Beneath the Beauty
The Tree-lined Street

anthologies
Playing in the Asphalt Garden
Shard I
Shard II
Burning Ambitions

DAMAGED

POEMS BY PHLIP ARIMA

DRAWINGS BY THOMAS HENDRY

INSOMNIAC PRESS

Edited by Mike O'Connor
Copy edited by Lloyd Davis & Liz Thorpe
Designed by Thomas Hendry & Phlip Arima
Readied for press by Mike O'Connor

Some of the poems in this collection have previously
appeared in the following publications: *Plus Zero*, *The Journal
of Literary Stuff*, *Scenes Magazine* and *Acta Victoriana*.

Canadian Cataloguing in Publication Data

Arima, Phlip, 1963-
         Damaged

Poems.
ISBN 1-895837-21-9

I. Title.

PS8551.R762D35 1998   C813'.54   C98-930290-X
PR9199.3.A74D35 1998

Printed and bound in Canada

The publisher and author gratefully acknowledge the support
of the Ontario Arts Council.

Insomniac Press
393 Shaw Street, Toronto, Ontario, Canada, M6J 2X4
www.insomniacpress.com

Table of contents

untitled — if tears could…   9
untitled — remember me…   11
untitled — we took off...   12
A.F.   14
Be Quiet   16
Ant Trails   18
He Does   20
Hit and Run — Basil —   22
Jane — waiting for the light to change   24
Push Not Pull   26
Dance baby dance   29
Rushing to Heaven   30
It will not make the news   32
Nigel   33
I take a breath   34
One Moment Free   37
As trains go by   38
Shriek   39
alone by the door   41
The Watcher Lonely   42
I would like   43
My eyes open   44
years   46
Looking for food   47
This stare   48
Shadows   49
untitled — Our last hug   51
09-06-96 Eulogy for Chris   52
Goodbye   60
Leaving the Mix   61
late at night   63
Without your voice   64
Not Going Anywhere   67
Swish   70
When everything…   72

After the Ecstasy   74
Here   75
In my room   76
Where is the Night   78
Father's Day   80
Listening   81
The Ache   82
Wednesday Morning   83
untitled — the lease on the sky...   84
Hello Hello   Where are you?   85
Notches   86
Summer   87
Not Hard Enough   89
Before Dawn   90
Delirious near sleep   91
monos   92
Growing   95
"No"   96
Take Thirty-Two   98
The imbecile cums as the clock strikes one   100
untitled — standing naked...   102

with love and special thanks to Faith Bisram
who saw me through the roughest night

if tears could make flowers grow
the world would be beautiful

Remember me in your grave
                    be it deep or shallow
        remember   why i gave

Remember me in your grave
                    turning over with rage
        remember   why i gave

Remember me in your grave
                    as the flowers wilt and decay
        remember   why i gave

Remember me in your grave
                    when the years make it silent
        remember   why i gave

we took off our clothes and ran
in the rain. a circle on the grass
at the back of the house. it was
dark out. most of the world was asleep.
the cars on the highway were hushed.
the jets beyond the clouds could barely
be heard.

we ran.

we ran until the circle was the only
track to follow. it became a deep rut
with smooth hardened sides. so high.
impossible to climb. always dark. filled
with harsh breathing and skin
calloused grey.

we ran.

we ran as the world changed and
as it remained. some children were
born. some of them died. the ones
that lived we taught all we had
learned.

they look up for the stars
more than we ever have.

A. F.

She cuts out all the eyes
from every picture in *chickadee*

colours over the hands
in dark purple crayon

says to me
now it looks righter.

Be Quiet

There's something different about the house. The kitchen looks the same. And the bathroom still smells like the can that sprays. But something has changed.

I was watching television, playing with my toys, when outside I heard the boys from next door. One was Darry, my friend. I went out to see what he was doing. When I came in, all my toys were put away, but no one was mad at me.

There's something different about the house. The stuff I'm not
supposed to touch in the back room is still leaning up against
the wall. There's laundry on the washer and some beside it
on the floor. But something, I don't know what, has changed.

After dinner, when Daddy went out, he didn't slam the door.
Mommy and me, we read a book. Halfway through
the phone rang. Mommy talked in a normal voice and
I even think I heard her laughing.

There's something different about the house. All the lights
still turn on and off. And the candles in the dining room
haven't been burned. But something has changed.

I'm going to go to sleep now, but you have to stay awake.
I'm going to sit you here, right beside my pillow. It's your job
to watch and see what bad things happen.

Ant Trails

lying in the grass counting ant trails
one begins at my right ankle, goes up the shin
then back again on a jagged crooked path

i don't know why they picked me
hit me, beat me to the ground and
ripped my clothes off

lying in the grass counting ant trails
another from under my arm goes to nipple
to belly to sex and down

they were three and big with hate
they spit, then swore, then cut me with a knife
when i cried they were happy, when i screamed
excited

lying in the grass counting ant trails
four circle my knee, two pass on my face
more move across my arms, ribs, hands, feet

when they entered me i went silent
shame shadowed the pain
the stabbing turned it black

lying in the grass counting ant trails
at eleven my focus fades

i want to move

He Does

a september dusk outside the mall
the boy in dark jeans   t-shirt
cotton jacket   bored   waiting
for the bus

the lights change   a car stops   the boy
looks in   an older man   scarred   ugly
smiles   points down the road   waves
for him to get in

he does

the man drives slowly   asks where the boy
is going   stops at another light   smiles
places a hand on the boy's thigh
drives

the boy lifts the hand away   it returns
closer to groin   firm   again
they stop   the boy asks   exactly
what the man wants

is answered   to get you off

the boy's junior-high parking lot   empty
now dark   his jeans below his knees
eyes shut   mouth still   listening to
the weather report

rough hands   wet mouth   moans
encouragement   demands   the boy
arches up   stiffens   releases   runs
from the car

Hit and Run   — Basil —

the man with the backward laugh

mixes his whisky with tears
sings songs with words nobody hears
dances and staggers off the edge of the curb

sees the light as he recognizes the screech and the curse
believes the life that passes is dust on dirt
does not cry with the pain or start at the shock

or think a significant thought
waiting for the rain, the siren, a someone
to hold him and say: rest easy, so long, bye bye.

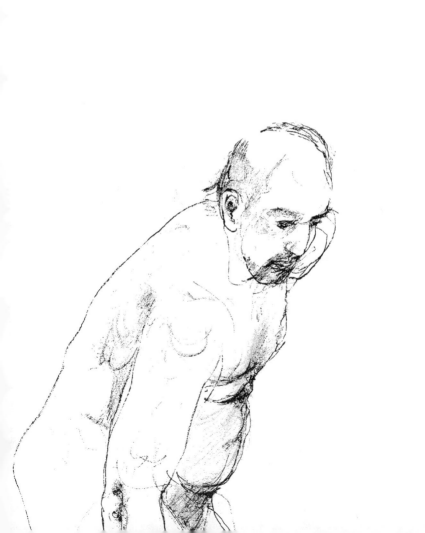

Jane — *waiting for the light to change* —

at the corner where cigarette filters cover the pavement
and little girls stoop to look through car windows
a woman smooths her hair back over her ear
waits for the light to change

she does not say a thing
as it goes from red to green to red again
then stepping out into the traffic her shrieks begin

"worthless fucking slut bitch   you don't deserve to live
take this   and this   and this   and this"

as the cars honk and swerve the hand repeatedly returns
to slap her face and turn the skin a swollen mauve
rip a lip so blood begins to flow

"worthless fucking slut bitch   you don't deserve to live"

the watchers seek each other out in eyes dry against the cold
see prophecy caught and denied as the woman
reaches the other side

she smooths her hair back over her ear
waits for the light
to change

Push Not Pull

I'm pushing my boxes across the street
there're eleven   but there were twelve
last night I reorganized everything
so it seems like there is less

I have to do this quickly
there's the traffic and there's people
once I was hit by a car then taken to the hospital
I was afraid all my things would be stolen

people are more dangerous than cars
I've had to fight with drunk ruffians
who thought they could harass me for fun
and sometimes when I sleep things go missing

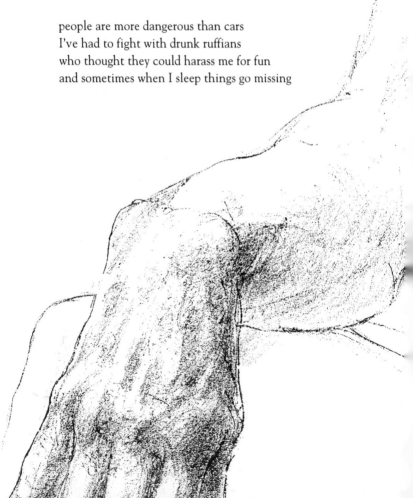

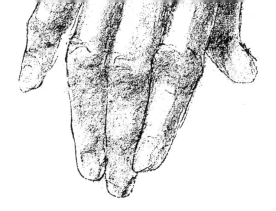

a man I don't know is asking to help
he's young but all right dressed so I tell him   yes
he starts pulling the box I've got halfway across
I have to stop him and explain the right way to do it

you gotta push not pull
pulling wears out the bottom too fast
makes the cardboard go soft at the corners
I'm glad he understands 'cause some cars are honking

the sky is getting dark and the wind picking up
soon it will be raining like all last week
if this man keeps helping
I'll be done before it starts

Dance baby dance

there is a rhythmic throb to the droning backdrop
of the many layers of memory complicating an event
so common it is no longer noted by the media
yet so real as to illuminate the despair
lurking within my thoughts

i am caught out on the tail end of two long hauls
with only a few hours sleep in between
half crashed   dropping off
into wonderless dream

the eyes   the nose   the mouth
and the skin over shattered cheekbones
are no longer a face as the light creeps out
of the swollen rawness that once craved life

too much knowledge gained in a single flash of insight
and i can hear my voice repeating   *dance*
baby dance   you ain't gonna cry blue no more
dance baby dance   you ain't gonna cry blue no more

Rushing to Heaven

Yuri climbs up the steps
to the thirty-first floor
takes his clothes off
and steps out a window

as he falls the city swirls
into a cylinder of glass
sharp electrical arcs
crisscrossing his path

the screaming of his voice
becomes the swoop of a sparrow
Yuri believes he is a god
shooting straight up to heaven

in his lungs he can taste sugar
mixed with ground ginger
as his skin turns to liquid
in an icicle sensation

seeing angels in neon
making love in wet orgies
Yuri ejaculates before he hits
the trunk of a car

It will not make the news

he leans out and lets go and falls
his eyes stay open and his mouth stays shut
and from a crack in the pavement
not far from where he hits
a ripe wild berry is trampled and crushed

and though some people are sickened
and others begin to pray
it will not make the news
perhaps because no one knows
his name nor from where he came

then again
maybe the berry is just a weed
a futile attempt to break the pavement
brighten the street

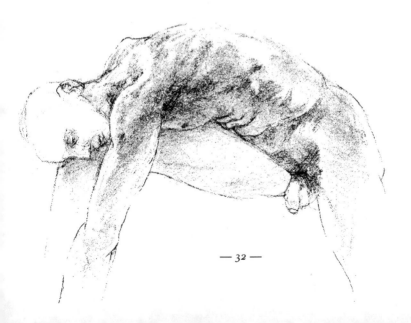

Nigel

i hear him talking to himself in the back of the bus
in a language i will never understand, wonder
what he carries in his pockets and his bag
know he wants another life to live

there are stories in his mind he can no longer tell
dreams he sold for something sadder than his smile
and as his shoes decay, he keeps waiting for that day
when the noise will be less loud

leaning against a locked door asking for change
he does not recognize me from five minutes before
looks as though he has never had a proper meal
knows how to survive a life i could not live

there are stories in his mind he can no longer tell
dreams he sold for something sadder than his smile
and as his shoes decay, he keeps waiting for that day
when the noise will be less loud

the buildings where he sleeps get torn down and redeveloped
while i warm my bed by making love surrounded by pillows
and sometimes when i look out my window, i see him on the street
know his hands have touched more life than i have lived

I take a breath

and i turn into a stone chipped from a building
and feet kick me to the street where car tires screech
and a kid picks me up to throw at a friend
and i bounce off a window not making a scratch
and i land in the garbage waiting to be collected
and in the middle of the night the trucks arrive
and i am taken to the dump where rats are fighting
and i am pushed underneath by giant bulldozers
and i turn into a man slowly exhaling.

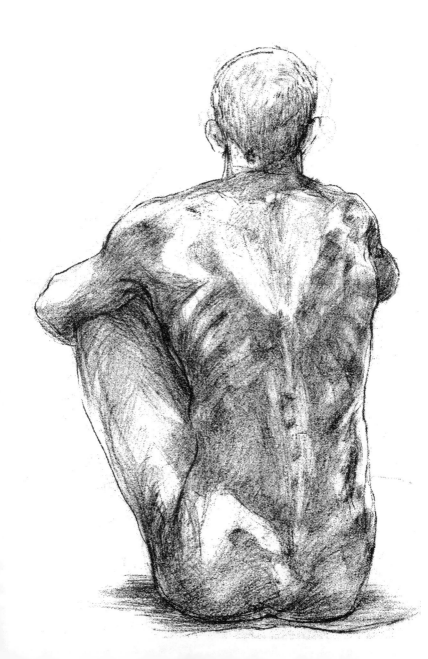

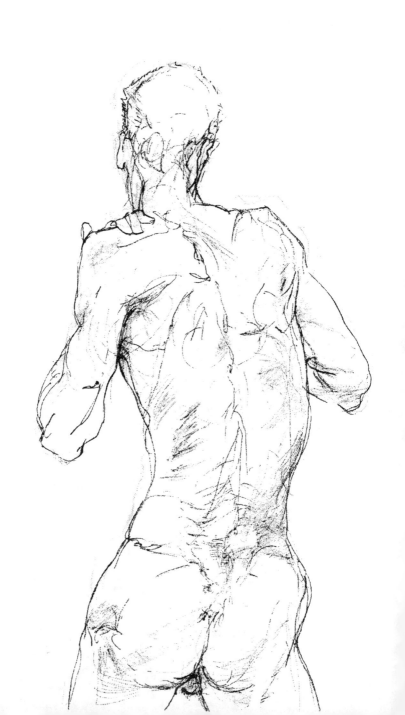

One Moment Free

i am walking down the street. slouched. head pulled to one side
by muscles that will not give up their hold. my feet drag, catch
in the cracks. every building i pass i have passed before.

a branch gets snagged between my fingers. i turn, fast. lash out,
palm flat. hit hard a post. the jolt goes to shoulder, to spine,
to guts, comes up. i am quickly pulled straight. my steps
hit the pavement like a large cat escaped.

at the corner i pause. look left, look right. look into the sky.
hear a swallow start to cry. sense the hollow in my lungs. feel
saliva on my teeth. taste a desire for flesh i cannot eat.

i close my eyes. let my skin expel heat. know the throb
in my throat is a rage i must hold. breath deep. count
until there is only an ache. slouch. open my eyes.
continue my walk down the street.

As trains go by

a bomb and an eye that has the world, horse stance,
violence, flesh tattooed and pierced while man blows horn
and monk strums lute, the school fool, wide-open child
and woman in white, rotten grin above the mic,

mask of death, head shaved, fingers in the air, dance
dance dance, hi daddy, soldier, freak on steps, freaks
in dump, nude, punk, head in a bag, crowd waving hands,
mother kissing child,

long legs in dress tight beneath a devil miniature,
skeleton, comic, filmmaker, three boys and a body,
buddha with walkman headphones on,
little girl smiling all scrunched up in a box

a shadowed heart, key chains, airplanes, a corpse,
rappers near a box, near a busker, near a pin-up and
a cure, the blues and a painted dude next to spacecraft
and monkey,

faces, blindness, a mushroom cloud.

Shriek

The brown glass of broken bottles
covers the cement wading pool
at the far end of the park.

The little girl takes off her shoes
and, skipping to an internal tune,
crosses the hazard without a cut.

A woman with a baby on her lap
touches her mouth and whispers soft:
miracle to the lord above.

All the others stand and stare
then as one voice begin to shriek
and shriek: *freak*.

alone by the door

one of four in the car   screeching
through the tunnel   wanting to scream
give voice to the pain   be like the sane
other three passengers on the train

screeching through the tunnel
like the rage on his brain   the fear
in his head   clawing its way
down his spine passed his ribs

to the core of his being   faster
than the train   screeching through
the tunnel   separate from the others
their loves and lovers

with his hands gripping tight   fixed
to the pole   turning rigid   turning
cold   as his legs start to shake
and muscles ache   and vision

turns grey   with no value at all
while the screeching through the tunnel
approaches the station   what he is calling
salvation

repeatedly saying   breathe man breathe
hang on and breathe   you just have to
make it   through the door to the platform
up the stairs to the street   and there

will be air   there will be air
not so many people   in so close a space
no more one of four   screeching
through the tunnel

wanting to scream   end a bad scene

The Watcher Lonely

night-time city   city street
through clouded glass thick with expelled human breath
see a child empty of dreams selling flowers

to a man who stands alone watching for someone to meet
make his life somehow complete   neat for him and his date
one he hopes will make the daily suck angelic

a fellow traveller bound to me by our lust for things to change
not like the coffee in my mug turning to a lukewarm sludge
nor the ashtray overflowing where a fire smoulders quiet

frigid flames in my lungs   shriek for silence in my head
i read a shirt in front of me stretched across a young kid's chest
flight!   the script looks like a slash in bloody thread
on cotton black

an icy blast from the doorway yanks me back out of myself
the watcher lonely has just entered   flowers breaking in his grip
petals falling to the muck and
dirty hopes lost by us

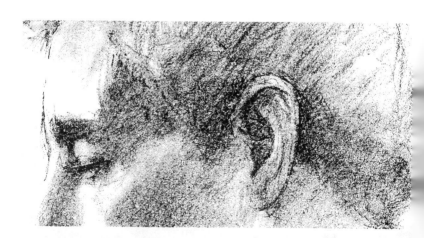

I would like

to laugh at the pedestrians scowling their faces
in shocked recognition of the desires they censor
as if touching their passion will cripple their souls

to stand on a tower and shout wild in the wind
so loud that no siren can drown out my voice
letting everyone know where the fire is exploding

to care about things so small they have meaning
like the scar of a piercing healed over for years
or a seed that starts sprouting before the ice is all melted

to hear light in the sky and see sound in the air
know a tear by its taste   a hair by its scent
a mood by the texture of sensitive skin

like a hero   like a lover   like a friend
touch mind to mind where there is no sense of time
realize all glory in a single moment of humility

be the nothing in everything   the wish in the dream
and no longer want to scream or plead for a change
ask for a hope or smile through death

I would like to watch the stars start to slide
the world spin in wonder and the universe expand
touching your fingers with mine.

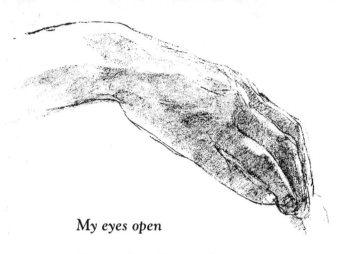

My eyes open

How long have I been awake?
breathing her heat? conscious of dreams?
thinking? remembering each pause
in the hours of conversation
before sleep?

Are there any cookies left?
has the lemonade soured? the flowers
wilted? does the meaning of all we said
still have relevance?

Is there anything I have to do?
calls to make? people to see? reason
not to caress her skin this overcast morning?

Was there a promise? will there be? what kind
of expectation still sleeps in the thin space
between our bodies?

Are the candles still burning? what was
the last song I heard? has the snow
started falling? can all that has happened
really have begun with a confession?

Did she say how long she would stay? does it matter?
do I care? will there be an obligation
when she opens her eyes and focuses on mine?

Was yesterday only a few hours ago?
do I have any food I can offer? any desire
I want satisfied? will she need me to be
more than I have been?

What time is it now? why must she leave?
where will she go? is the closeness we have shared
a gift she will carry? do I want to light a cigarette
and watch the smoke lift and get lost
on its way to the ceiling?

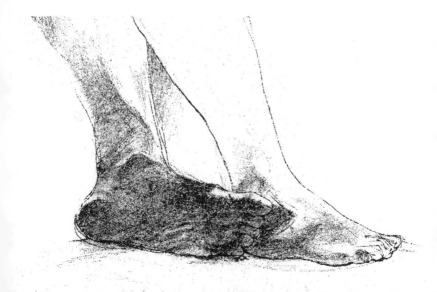

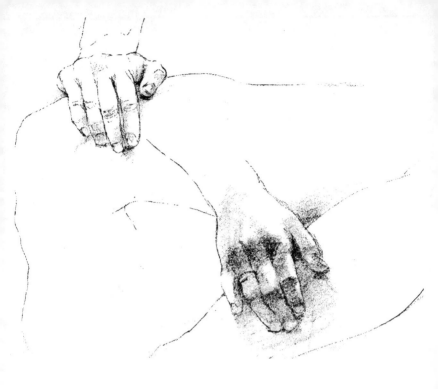

years

and with orgasm there are tears
the strength that draws no longer frightens
joy rushes through the consummation of a decade's desire
and the realization that too much has changed
pierces the space that cannot be named

"I love you" echoing without voice

Looking for food

they are fighters in the ring   they are soldiers in the field
it is noon on the first day after fifteen of rain

the trees are dropping the gold they got for green
he looks out the window and rethinks what he said

they are cannibals and lovers and too hungry to chew
the pollution and the iron and the brick will not change

smoke in the sun   cracker crumbs on the bed
in the distance two voices throw stones from their heads

a cat attacks a garbage can
looking for food

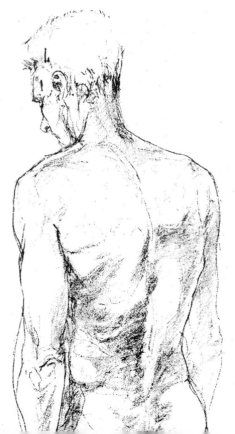

This stare

it is a stare, a stare so solidly fixed
that to change its perception demands
the sharpest possible ice pick

                but

it is not the stare of a hungry man
setting a snare and stoking a fire
impatiently waiting to satisfy desire

and it is not the stare of an anxious youth
hoping to define himself within another
then run away when he has gained some power

and it is not the stare of an awestruck boy
who has no history and only knows
what his father has told him

it is a stare, the stare of a single soul
ready to stand with you

Shadows

Standing in the middle of the road
looking beyond the buildings at the sun
i hold my hand up as if to stop traffic
and its red still hits me in the eye

turning thoughts of rubbish in the wind
to shadows creeping through my spine
in a convoluted game of hide and seek
with memories that will not sleep.

Standing alone in the late afternoon
looking beyond the buildings at the sun
as it descends on the horizon
like it is drained and done

when the catering truck horn sounds
louder and for longer than necessary
and i remember how much you liked
the chocolate doughnuts i will buy.

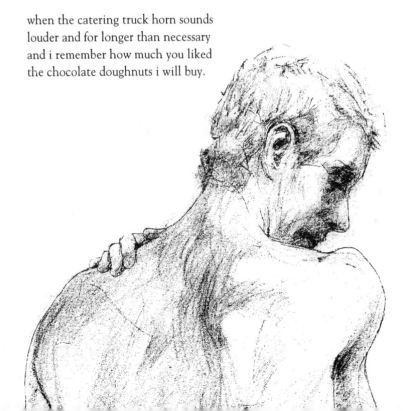

Our last hug locked up like a seatbelt in a head-on crash
the future was mapped when the outfit was bought

if you had turned into the skid the spin might have stopped
staring at the broken line all control was lost

I heard your scream from too far off
felt the collision arrest your heart

looking at my arm where your fingers gripped
I wish you had told me how far you were going.

09-06-96   *Eulogy For Chris*

She did not fear death
she hated him

every time a dream hit the dirt
no matter how hard she worked

when friendship would end
because she could not let you in

as she had a drink to take the edge off
and the next one and the next one called

at that moment of disappointment
before the pin went in
she hated him

is it over

yes...

a scene in the late-night movie
a syringe to a vein
the plunger pulled back
the blood   injection

...you can look now

it was the needle not the drug
i loved. when i was little and
so much in the hospital
they would bribe me with presents
candy and things if i would be
a brave little girl and let them
stick it in

another scene
should we change the channel

no   just tell me when it's over

remember the first time we dyed my hair
finding colours for weeks all over the bathroom
laughing

you never could get an omelette right
but your chocolate chip cookies
out of sight

always thought it funny
when you'd find me still awake at the desk
when you woke for work at five a.m.

no matter how angry, we never hit each other
that was rule number one and explains
the cracked walls in our first apartment

my old leather jacket too big for you
your thigh-high boots and helmet in hand
you looked so cool-cute   waiting for me

"boys and their toys"   "good boy"
i could always hear the affection
hidden in your sarcasm

remember the camp-out in new york
and walking through the mud
singing "i'm sticking with you"

i didn't like it when you drank
i liked it less that i knew
i could not stop you

when i'd read you to sleep with winnie-the-pooh
curled up holding your stuffed animal, boo
you looked so innocent and in peace

you survived the streets
built a home for yourself
understood what it meant to have respect

i didn't know how to play when i met you
couldn't trust too well either
you taught me a lot

i loved you

still do

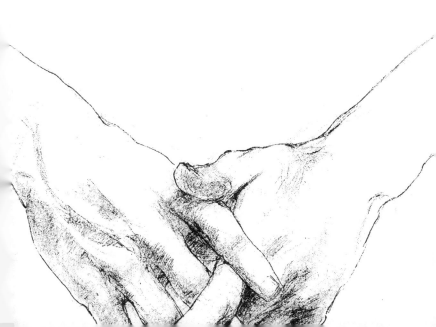

the funeral processions that pass on the street,
news stories of tragic loss, demonstrative statistics,
local gossip, songs about all the people who died
died out on a mainline

                          did not prepare me,
ease the angst of your life disappearing
with a needle by your bed.

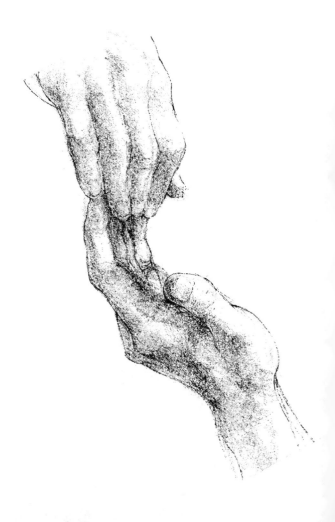

we were a couple before we were roommates
one ended, there was some space, the other began

seven years minus three months we lived together
learned each other's buttons and refused to push them

not expecting, always surprised, i would trip
over easter eggs or halloween candy left outside my door

spiders and other nasty bugs were my job
mowing the lawn and taking the garbage out, hers

she would cut my hair, and i would play fashion consultant
and we shopped together for all kinds of things

trading cards, comics, pictures, clothing, furniture
we had a hell of a time hauling the microwave home

and at our place in the annex
we covered a wall with posters pulled from bloor

and at our place near christie and st. clair
we had a beautiful backyard we never used

and that winter in between, too close to scarborough
we survived eight weeks in a basement bachelor

we laughed, we cried, we tried, we cared
we dared to work and make life good

once, early on, after making love, i asked, "are we doing
all right?" and she answered, "i'm still here, aren't i?"

"it's eleven o'clock. do you know where your parents are?
nope." then she would fix her lunch and put herself to bed

she told me she said that to the room when she was fourteen years old
she told me they told her — be back by eleven or don't come home

two years later, nearing nineteen, she learned
they did not mean what they had said

"pay the extra forty. i'm really bad at head"
later she was proud of more than her ability to fuck

she would be there for others no matter what
but never got the hang of letting them close

it was as if she lived behind a two-way mirror
and you only knew she was there by her laughter

not her tears

oh, baby...   little one...

i'm glad you knew i was here for you
sad you could not reach out, let me further in

please know this — i am not angry at you
and i understand what took you down

it seems like you got kicked in the head
every time you almost turned it around

you did some amazing things
made a lot of lives a little brighter

you let me learn to love.

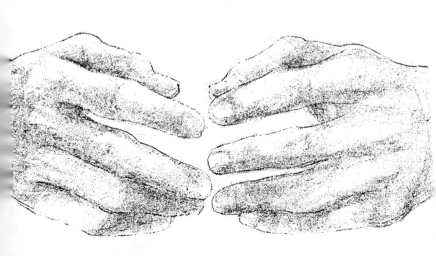

Goodbye

I watch a breath on the wind
its sentiment is deeper   darker
less travelled   less lost
than the force with which it flies

I watch a breath on the wind
its moisture is thick
with the sweetness of a heart
opening like a mouth
closing over a nipple

I watch a breath on the wind
in a time when no war
turns my thoughts into knives
that can hack but not slice

I watch a breath on the wind
long before i am waking
to this wet city morning
as car tires shift the flow
of water across pavement

Leaving the Mix

when the lonely descends like locusts across ripe land
and the stuff from the pharmacist hasn't the kick
i want to leave the mix

every breath is a reminder; every thought a question
i don't expect to feel better, just nothing and numb
out of the mix

your hand blistering on mine as you watch me decay
with what is left of my heart i wish you would look away
somewhere besides this edge of the mix

late at night

there are moments of endless length
when the noise is not so loud, when the ache
does not seem like pain, when i do not feel
like you abandoned me, gave up while i
continue the struggle.

they are soft moments i fill with candlelight
forgiveness and reflection. moments when i
can exhale each breath without the sadness
crippling me — turning my eyes
liquid grey.

moments when i can accept your death
and all the little daily deaths as part
of my life, a life that has these
quiet moments of alone.

Without your voice

i want to talk to you.
you see, i'm in that space
where shadows sway on asphalt grey.
nothing to point at and say: there,
that's the dagger coming on
end over end, sure to sink sharp
into my skin. nothing to grab either,
nothing big enough to hang on to.
no rocket ready to launch, just
glowing coals needing me
to keep blowing.

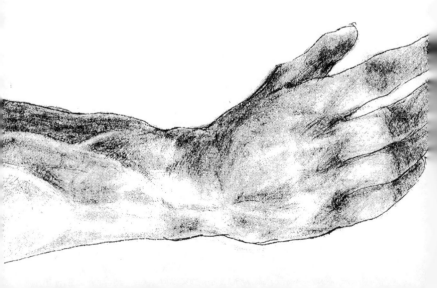

i want to talk to you.
i'm in that space i keep coming to:
no eat, no sleep, no dream. sure,
i swallow. it's mechanical. and i
spend time unconscious. and there's
things i crave. but the sea is a mirror
and the engine is cranked way over
so i just keep spinning 'round
and 'round, bouncing off
my own wake.

I want to talk to you.
hear you say: it'll be okay,
you never bleed for too long,
never don't come up for air
even when you touch bottom
with the ship. i know all this
but without your voice
the words are colourful kites
broken from their strings.

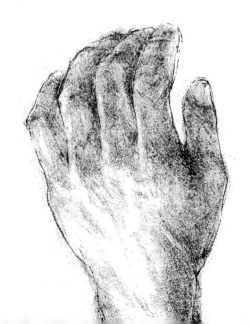

Not Going Anywhere

— where ya been? — gimme a break. i been busy. — busy.
fuck. gimme a break. it wasn't like i could call 411 and get
your number. — i said i was busy, okay? deal with it.
— believe me, i am. — me too. — why? what's going on?
— paperwork. forms to fill out. line-ups like you wouldn't
believe. and you can't just call. you have to show up in
person. it's really ignorant. — stupid. — whatever. — why
can't you call? — there's no telephones. you gotta, kinda
think the connection. it's hard to explain. — try. — trust
me, you don't want to know. — yes i do. — well, i don't
want to try and explain it. — fine.

— anyway, you gotta know who you want to talk to.
actually know them. and if they don't want to talk to you,
they just block you out. — block you out? — yeah, block
you out. it's a pain. i'm only now starting to get the hang of
it. you're my first long distance. — really? — yeah, well, it
wasn't too hard 'cause i know you so well. — that's for sure.
— yeah. you know… you know, i'm sorry. — i know.
i am too. it's all right. — did you get something of mine?

— i got your lighter. — the grandfather one? — of course.
— good boy. it's the one with the spare flint holder.
— i know. i remember when you showed it to me. — are
you going to engrave it? — maybe. when i get some money.
— cool. — but on the inside. on the part that pulls out.
— why not on the outside, on the back. — because i don't
want to. all right? — all right. — look, i'll know. it's not
like i'm going to forget you. — i know.

— so what's it like there? you got a nice place? — it's all right. it's fucking crowded here. but i got my own shower. and it's so cool how the showers work. you can move the spray to hit you from any direction and there's no hose and you don't have to hold anything and the pressure is amazing and you never run out of hot. never! — good. you deserve it. — and, oh, you know what else? — what? — my teeth are fixed.

— what about your back? — it still hurts some. but it's a lot better. — drag. — yeah. — do you have your own kitchen too? — we don't eat here. — you don't? — nope. — not even chocolate? — i haven't found any yet. — can you smoke? — designated areas only. — figures. — doesn't it. and they don't have my brand either. — nothing's perfect. — no kidding.— so what do you do? — watch t.v. — no, i mean what are you going to do? you'll go nuts without work. — i know. — so? — so? — so what are you going to do? — i don't know. i don't think there is anything to do. — don't they have plants, gardens? — yeah, but. . . — but you need a certificate or a licence or something. — right. — can you relocate?

— well, i could come back. — you can? are you going to?
— no. — why not? — the line-up's too long. i mean it's
really long. and then i'd have to live again. — you could
do it. i know you can. — i don't want to. — okay. it's
just… it's just, i still believe in you. — but i don't know
that i do. — well try. — we'll see. — yeah, i guess we
will. — anyway, i don't have anything more to say.
— okay. are you going to call again? — probably.
i'm not going anywhere.

Swish

there is a window
around the screen
a scream in the bean
that rattle rattle rattles
as the shoulders go roll
with each stride down the road

so say the words that take nerve
see the comic tricks happen
to the stoic expressions
pushing through life
like a high-speed disaster

or swish or wish
or be crazy kill happy
and ask the strange question
is "if" a prerequisite or just a bad habit
like bureaucratic confetti
at an orgiastic reception

tingle tie why
tie ting   sigh lie
my boots are too high
and the gloves on my hands
have no ends to their fingers
but the hat on my head
keeps the brain pan from dead

and that window up above
could be a funky kind of love
letting mosquitoes come in
under dragonfly wings

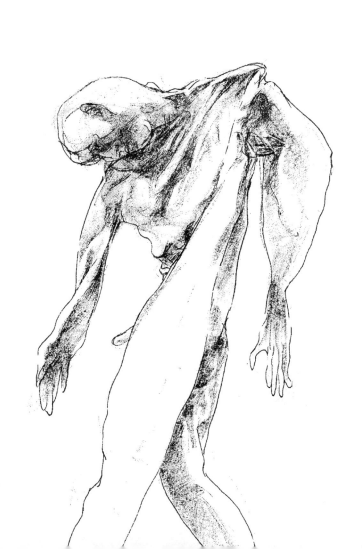

When everything...

when everything starts happening
it will be midnight or three

cell-phones and beepers and piercings to conform
a guy is going to be branded as part of the show
when it's over there'll be a dj all the way from L.A.

when everything starts happening
it will be difficult to breathe

last week there were five fights that nobody won
the bouncers threw them out before they were done
and some people who wore white were too stupid to leave

when everything starts happening
it has to be seen

they sell beer in the back at five dollars a can
and that woman in the hat has the best drugs around
if this is a good night someone famous will be here

when everything starts happening
you will not remember my name

After the Ecstasy

i take a mouthful of water
i so want to swallow

hold my lips over yours
let you drink

as the sweat starts to dry
exhaustion sedates

words take on a gentle shape
while meaning disappears

in the emotion we communicate
as the city awakes

and our tongues relax
silent sleep

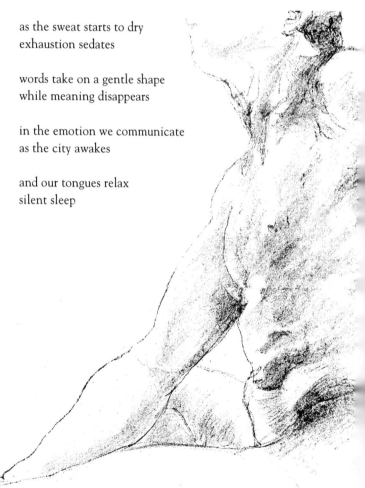

Here

i am thick and i am thin and i am tight and i am flat
and i am blitzed and groovy and rushing the edge
and grasping the answer to the question
that cannot be asked   here

is the where i stop swallowing the myth
here is the where i dance and i strip

this is the space where this kid lost his head
on that occasion of strangeness
when the funniest thing was the attempt to explain
the funniest thing   and i realized

the startling truth that everything is nothing
and nothing the sum of all that there is

                    here

where if i think i am living i am actually dead

In my room

there is an animal alive in my room.
i cannot see it. i cannot hear it.
but i know it. know it is alive.
alive in my room.

i am sitting in the corner on the floor.
my back to the walls. i am in my room.
my empty room. wrapped naked in a blanket
i found in the hall.

there is an animal alive in this room.
i sense it. i dislike it.
i want it to leave before i capture
and kill it.

beyond the window there is wind.
a wind silenced by fog. fog glowing cool
with a power i crave. a power
i can use.

there is an animal alive in the room.
it is beginning to move. it knows
how to chew. it breathes with a rhythm
that reflects my own.

i am sitting on the floor looking up
at the bare bulb. it brightens
as its filament burns out. leaving me
in doubt.

there is an animal alive in its room.
it is alone. and it is angry. and it is happy.
so happy its growl can be felt
as it swallows.

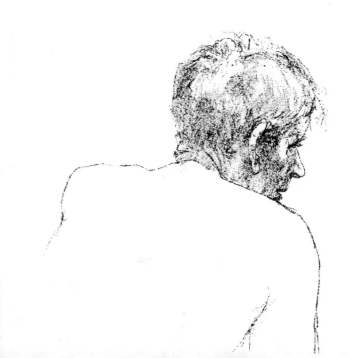

Where is the Night

Why is it so bright?
i used to lie on the sharp stones between the tracks
near my home

How can I tell the nasty shadows from the friendly ones?
i could see the rail on my left or on my right,
but not both at the same time

Did I just hear something?
usually i stared straight
into the sky

Is there someone there?
it felt best when it was cool
and the stars seemed real close

Will things ever be dark like they were?
when a train shook the earth and the cars
flew past my face, i would scream

Why is there the taste of metal in my mouth?
i would scream from a hidden place
deep down inside

What is going to happen if I let loose a shout?
more than once two trains would go by
at the same time

Is anyone near enough to hear?
the sky would become a strip
no wider than my head

Does the soul have a mind of its own?
my body would arch up as i writhed and it felt
like blood was running from my eyes

Are the crazy the sane?
the power of cold steel on cold steel
was all i could hear

Why are the shadows always dressed in white?

Father's Day

once upon a time there was time to talk
i remember a scene from hospital dark

with death hand reaching he asked for forgiveness
with rage increasing i gave as expected

i hear a little kid crying in the park
once upon a time i had an open heart

Listening

the telling of a life story late at night
with an injured hand lying limp
on a pillow stained with spunk
and no sound except the furnace
blowing dry air for a few seconds
at the end of each year

words spoken in the same tone
emergency ward doctors use
when speaking amongst themselves
as if this will render the events
less real and more easily
understood

words spoken with only one listener
half revealed by the street light
filtering through a window
as i toy with a doll
beside a mattress on the floor
that has never been for sleeping

words spoken so slowly and so honestly
and with such credible detail
that though no thoughts
fill my mouth
i fall into a pit
where all i can feel is love

The Ache

It is a tiny room
with no windows   white walls
nightmares by the locked door

the skin crawls

It is a place filled with smoke
hard light   emotions that strike
and dry blood on the rim of an eye

the stomach cramps

It is a place i stay
at the bad hours of the day
when the chill makes the crowd too dense

the hands clench

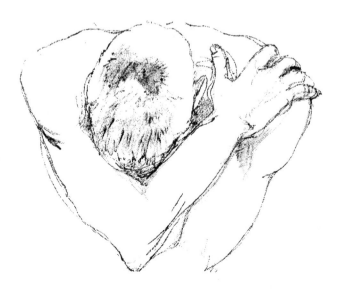

Wednesday Morning

cold air blows through the crack in the window
killing the candle that lit the night

a dog is barking

the scarves that hang from the foot of the bed
have left their mark in my flesh

the sheets are wet

before you fell asleep you said: i love you
and all i could think of was death

the lease on the sky has run out
yesterday was the last day of blue

i am looking at my reflection
from the inside of a phone booth
and the rain is running tears from my eyes

by morning it will all ice over
the memory of your voice will be frozen

Hello Hello   Where are you?

it's raining black drops of perspiration from a dirty god
the trees though do not seem to mind   they thrive
thrive   they are alive   and green   are we

i saw your name in a restaurant john stall
should i have added your number   do you even have
a phone   i dial and dial and all i get is a tone

it's raining black drops of perspiration from a dirty god
the cars though do not seem to mind   they multiply
multiply   are they alive

last week when we spoke you had a book full of words
i do not know   can you teach me to say the things
you read

it's raining black drops of perspiration from a dirty god
but the dj on 89.1 does not seem to mind   he's playing
every one of our favourite songs   favourite songs

if you are listening
it's kinda like we are
together

Notches

we are dancing to the tune of a computer-generated song
our feet do not shuffle and our bodies do not sway
and we each want to ask what the other considers love

if you take off your clothes in front of me tonight
i will pretend to be impressed or at least fake excitement

we are walking down the street holding hands in the dark
speaking in circles about where we are going
looking for avenues that might not dead end

if i take off my clothes in front of you tonight
will you definitely be grateful and promise discretion

we are waking in the morning exhausted and uncomfortable
the day is too fresh and the coffee too weak

here is my number, i hope you lose it.

Summer

I sit beside the swings in the playground
    everything is concrete with people hanging in the heat
    as peeling paint falls from the highest balconies
    like soot-coloured snow that will never melt
while children learn to bite and scratch in a fight
    the air smells of garbage and car exhaust
    and stray dogs scroung for something to eat
    or chase after cats that always escape
knowing this place is home to hunger and hate.

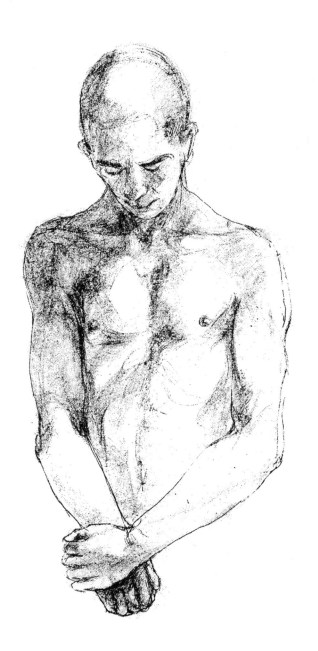

Not Hard Enough

The children with fathers who do not know their names
    search for wedding rings and laughter and cinnamon sunsets
    drive the centre lane in a rusting away dream

    turn left at the corner where the sign says no right
    as she whispers in his ear, my daddy will not like you
    you're not hard enough… not hard enough.

The children with fathers who do not know their names
    race to find their place within the great game
    eat popcorn and coke and chocolate-covered candy

    make love with their lust and teenage anxiety
    imagine all the roads run straight through the night
    and that the songs on the radio tell the truth about life.

The children with fathers who do not know their names
    religiously buy lottery tickets twice every week
    always believe their numbers will win.

Before Dawn

you asleep on your bed
me by the door on the floor
the light of television touching our skin

your body quiet
hands still   face soft
we share your dreams when you talk

you wake up and turn it off
no words are spoken in the dark
we get dressed   go for a walk

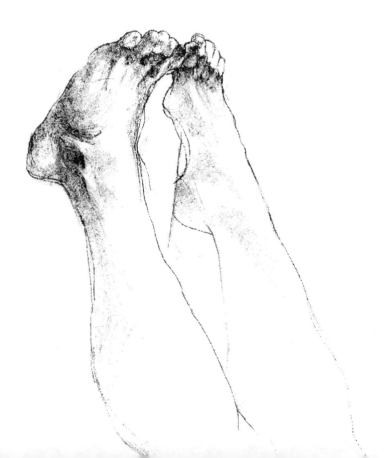

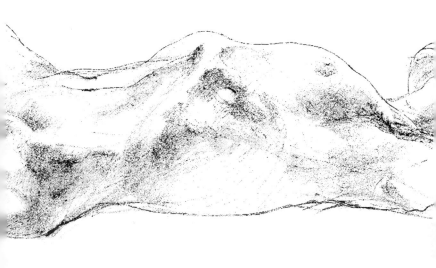

Delirious near sleep

a teardrop shadow on your throat
the metronome of my heart speaking with the dark

every seven cuts the song comes around
to let you repeat   this one is deep

and i sigh into you each time i agree
such sadness is beauty.

monos

watching a body crippled by a face that winked   smiled
turned to a shadow and flew through the stone structure
of a building too tall to climb

when we kissed there was blood   it coloured our eyes
then drained through our guts

i saw a dog die in the heat   as it fell it tried to growl
the sound was not unlike our breathing after we were done

when the days are dark with storm   and the nights clear
i feel the blood we share

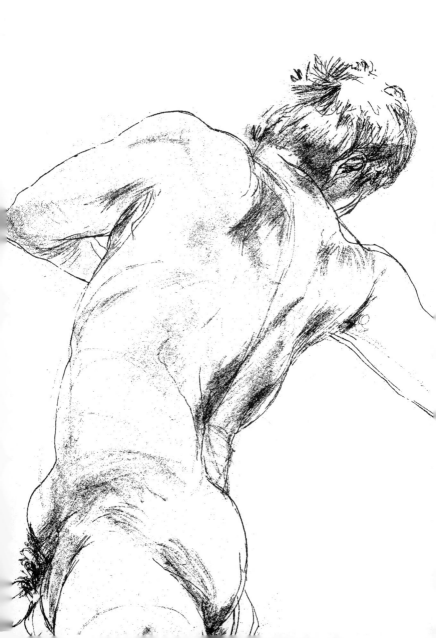

Growing

i wake up. grey. a fuzzy day. combination of street light, daylight, intermittent light from the auto shop sign. good to have a room with a window above ground. did my time in quiet darkened basement. deserve luxury. see the two tallest branches of my palm. where they fork a leaf. i watch it grow. it is slow. the bed vibrates. the train is loud. sitting up i can see: cp rail. cp rail. cp rail. hear bird noises: not necessarily singing. could be conversation. argument. too many individuals talking to themselves all at once. time is a difficult concept. i have two clocks. neither ever agree. i stand and stretch: shoulder blades. neck. knees and toes. knees and toes. knees and toes. i have to sneeze. don't, though. also an itch inside my throat. water. swallow. good to have a glass by the bed. children have to use plastic cups. did my time. a difficult concept. dogs are barking. could be singing. could be talking. i can't remember when i last spoke with anyone. could call 411. say hello. don't though. coffee. thank you. short conversation with myself. no milk. oh, well. think it is wednesday. could be thursday. NOW. do dishes. take coffee back to room. sit at desk. the light is different. the leaf still grows. slow. i hit the power on computer. remember when i did not wake alone. did the motions just the same: coffee. knees and toes. watch the glow. different, though. conversation: morning. good morning. dream? tell. often singing. never barking. yet two palm branches parting. the search for light. thirst for water. change. space. time. a difficult concept. all new leaves start off pale. sip at coffee. burn tongue. blow, blow, blow. call 411. get her number. still the same. want to dial. don't, though.

"No"

The snow has melted to water
and, warming in the heat,
clings to the surface of her hair.
It does not run or drip
and is a long way from the next step:
evaporation.   It is trapped
by the force in all objects
that attracts one thing to another
regardless of their life
or lifelessness.   It waits
as if it can dictate
what will next take place
when, with a shake of her head,
the connection is broken
and those few drops of moisture
are gone.

Take Thirty-Two

I have been told that when the ground freezes
           landmines will explode
                          I feel so cold

          a slow pan across the crowd finishing with a tilt
everyone looks great in the dark   she won't be a bit
     of a junky for long   hair burning on the washroom floor
the ambulance operator puts us on hold   the priest is packing
                     to move out of the city

                                         we are caught in the spotlight
                              we are craving cherry lip balm
                     we are wearing tinted glasses and advertising clothing
               we are the majority of society and a danger to ourselves

          waiting for the zoom
to make the effects perfect

                                         waiting for the zoom
                              to make the effects perfect

as the furnace is burning   as the flowers are wilting
as the pictures all curl   as memories merge
as eyes are lost in diminishing thought

a backwash of basil with a red pepper thread
        I want to shut down the out-of-sync tick
                powder polished stones   pour oil in water
                        tell those who keep calling I no longer laugh

                got a tube to my jugular   got a tube to my lungs
        got a tube to my stomach   got a tube to my heart
got a tube to the sewers that are managed by the city

        the toys fell apart   the toys fell apart
                I hear voices repeating identical phrases
                        sugar in coffee leaves the colour the same
                                a machine is here to record your message

The imbecile cums as the clock strikes one

This is where we walk. slowly or quickly,
it does not matter. our direction can have end
or be mindless wandering. if we breathe,
we cannot be free.

There is an imbecile on the steps of the government building.
he watches our every move. in the daytime when the sunshine
filters through the world's waste, he calculates. at night,
as we live the life, he masturbates.

In a room not too far to the north and east
a cigarette is lit with beer-wet lips, a song from the sixties
rotates on the turntable, and a woman wonders why
she no longer wants to cry.

From the stool next to mine, a man tells a story.
his listeners nod agreement then refocus
on the screen. the bartender smiles,
pours drinks, counts tips.

There is a moan in the still, a tourniquet on desire.
hands grow arthritic. eyes lose to cataracts.
breath mints can be bought
for less than a dollar.

standing naked in winter rain
hearing the noise whisper its threat

running lonely through dark
listening for a voice to follow

breathing like everyone else
because that is what i know

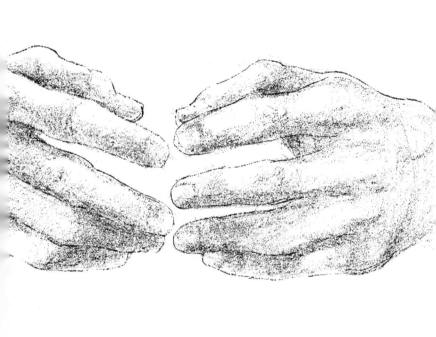

About the Drawings:

The images reproduced in this volume are taken from two suites of work produced during 1997 and 1998. The first is a continuing series of figure drawings; the other a suite of drawings provisionally titled "deflations". Both sets of work consist of indian ink on Japanese paper.

A number of the original drawings are available for purchase. For further information please contact the artist through Insomniac Press.

A Note of Thanks:

Special thanks has to be extended to Phlip and to all the individuals who provided the catalyst for the drawings. Toronto is blessed with a large and very professional community of artist's models, without whose patience and professionalism these pieces could not exist.

Particular thanks must be extended to those friends and models whose images add to the human landscape of this volume. Thanks again to:

Michael, Falcon, Julie, Michelle, Jackie, Corinne, King, Abelardo, and all the others.

And above all, many thanks to Murray Mackay, a pro among pros.

Thanks also to Mark, Dave, Paul and the staff of the Toronto School of Art, under whose roof many of these drawings first came to light.

— T.H., FEB. 1998

PRINTED AND BOUND
IN BOUCHERVILLE, QUÉBEC, CANADA
BY MARC VEILLEUX IMPRIMEUR INC.
IN APRIL, 1998